YOU'RE NO BODY 'TIL SOMEBODY
KILLS YOU

Peggy Cartmill Insula

You're No Body 'til Somebody Kills You

Dedicated to
My husband, Eugenio
My children, Valerie, Travis, and Wheat
My grandchildren Danielle, Michael, Savannah,
and Zander

Retirement was Hell. Maggie sighed and sank deeper into her lawn chair. No worries, no responsibilities, freedom at last. The condo behind her stood tall and quiet, still sleeping at the end of sunrise. Cool spring breezes flowed over her skin. Delightful. Gentle, early morning sun rays bathed her as murmurs from the unhurried river beyond the nearby sea wall soothed her weary soul. Thank God for Florida. She could stay right where she was forever. The river sang its lullaby. Maggie dozed a few feet from its edge.

A niggling sensation pricked at her consciousness. She passed a hand over her face to brush it away. Like a fly, the annoying tickle persisted. "Pay attention," it seemed to say.

She sat up. The melody of the river took on an urgent tone. There, six feet from the edge, a bloated male body floated face down. The water beyond him rippled, and two soulless yellow eyes emerged. The alligator waited, unhurried as the river.

"Oh my God," Maggie said. "I knew Old Greensides would take one of those foolhardy waders."

Sooner or later, it had to happen. Tourists. They thought they were fishing at a fish farm.

She rose from her chair and walked to the sea wall. She clasped her face in both hands and held her breath. The nine-foot alligator rippled the water with slow, cat-like switches of its tail. Its eyes gleamed. Lazily, it glided forward, inches from the body. Maggie gritted her teeth and braced herself for the horrible attack. The gator paused, lifted its giant head, and submerged. The theme from *Jaws* played in Maggie's head. Seconds—or was it hours—later it surfaced between the corpse and the sea wall. Maggie stood rooted to the spot. The police, she needed to call the police. The gator lay as still as the body floating beside it. One yellow eye fixed on the corpse, the other on Maggie. She shivered and tore her gaze away from the horrid sight, only to turn back to the scene that both repulsed and fascinated her.

The back of the guy's balding head looked familiar. Could it be? She craned her neck and scanned his clothing. White tee-shirt, khaki pants worn too low. Her hateful neighbor, Chuck Sweeney. He hadn't changed his clothes. She had just had a confrontation with him last night about her leaving the pool gate open for five seconds while she fetched a towel from her car, parked right in front of the pool. Overbearing control freak.

Unreal. None of this was real. Maggie pinched herself and headed to her second-floor condo to call the police. Of all the people who wanted him dead, it had to be an alligator who took him out. She shook her head at the irony. Had Sweeney tried to tell Old Greensides his rules for the river?

***

She placed her call and waited on the glider on the patio. Below her the river slosh, sloshed against the sea wall. Old Greensides had disappeared, lurking, probably. Taking his time to plan his assault.

Maggie wrapped her arms around her chest and moved the glider slowly. So much for a trouble-free retirement. Was it less than an hour ago that she lay congratulating herself about never again needing to drag herself up too early and trudge off to work?

She mustn't think about the alligator. Work. Think about work, Maggie. Her last three years had been miserable. It wasn't the children she taught. She loved them. Most of the time, anyway. Although they could be imps... Was that the gator's tail making those ripples at the dead man's head? Maggie shook herself... It wasn't the parents either. One of her strengths was her ability to form good relationships with parents. It wasn't even the inane administrative tasks or pressures about testing and accountability. No, she had to admit it was her own decline in stamina, energy, and general health. She just didn't have what it took to meet the demands of her job any more. Well, there'd be no need to sweat that now. Now all she had to think about was... dead bodies and alligators.

The door to the patio of the condo below her slammed, and a shrieking, bleached-blond, middle-aged woman ran onto the grass, waving her arms. "Oh, my God!" she screamed. "Oh, Lord, it's a dead body right at my doorstep. Help me, somebody, help me." She crumpled to her knees.

"For Heaven's sake, Naomi, shut up." Maggie jumped from the glider and placed her hands on her hips. "Pull yourself together before you alarm the whole neighborhood."

Naomi, now on her hands and knees, gasped but stopped her caterwauling. "Do...do you know who it is?"

"Yes. It's one of your boyfriends. It's Chuck Sweeney. The alligator got him."

Wrong thing to say. This brought on another round of wailing.

"If you don't shut your mouth right now, Naomi, I'll tell the whole condo community all about your 'secret' visits to him when his wife was away."

Naomi lifted her head to glare at Maggie. "Why, you meddlesome old hag," she hissed.

"Look, Naomi. I don't give a damn what you do. I just want you to close your big mouth before you alarm everybody within five miles. The deputy sheriff won't appreciate you disturbing the scene. Now, get your sorry ass up and go back inside."

Naomi stood, muttered "Oh, my, oh, my, oh, my," sniffed, wrung her hands, but dragged herself back into her unit.

***

The sheriff's department arrived. Grateful for the box seat view that living on the second floor afforded her, Maggie sat upright in her glider while they examined the scene. A tall, burly man in the green county uniform swaggered over to the sea wall, stood with his hands on his hips, and stared at the body.

Obvious from his confident manner, he was the officer in charge. A high-ranking detective, Maggie guessed. Now and then he shook his head. No need to check closer to affirm death. Three other officers, young rookies, flanked him and cast ashen, uncertain glances in his direction. Still no sign of Old Greensides. Should she warn them about him? No. The dispatcher had no doubt given them that information.

The big man turned and walked slowly along the sea wall. His eyes searched the grass on the verge of the wall. Once he looked up abruptly and met Maggie's eyes for a moment before returning to his search.

He stopped and knelt for a closer look at the grass. He motioned to the others. "Jones, Ferguson, get over here."

The two new-looking, reedy officers, one black and one white, lurched over to him. One held his stomach; the other had his hand to his mouth. Maggie waited for them to toss their cookies. From the looks of them, this was their first death investigation. Why wasn't she nauseated? She pinched herself again.

The detective rested his elbows on his knees and pointed to the grass beside him. "Here's where the body was dragged into the river. Follow this and see where it takes you. Don't mess up the trail."

Maggie took a deep breath. My God. Had Old Greensides come out of the water to take his prey? He sure was one calculating reptilian beast.

"You don't think he drowned, then?" Ferguson scratched his head.

The detective stood. "Oh, no. The trail heads toward the condos. An alligator wouldn't hunt that far from the river. The victim was killed somewhere else and dragged here."

Maggie gasped.

The rookies nodded and searched, one on each side of the flattened grass that made a faint path across the lawn. Or so Maggie assumed. Her vision began to fail her as the men followed the path into the distance. Their movements appeared more confident now that they had an assignment.

The detective strolled back to his remaining man. "Kinsey, find the tarp. We have to fish this guy out. The coroner isn't going to wade into the river to examine him."

Kinsey, another slender young man—where did the county find them all—strode off toward the cars in the parking lot.

The detective surveyed the condos while he waited. Maggie would have bet that eyes peered out of every unit. One old guy walked up from the other building, but the detective waved him off before he got within fifty feet. The man turned and waddled back toward his unit.

Taking his cell phone from his belt, the detective called for an ambulance.

Kinsey returned with two pairs of waders and a tarp. His movements were efficient, matter-of-fact. Maggie studied him. He must be made of sterner stuff than the other two. The men pulled the waders on over their uniforms, sat on the sea wall, and dropped into the knee-deep water. They slogged over to the corpse and slipped the tarp under his body, enveloping it like a taco. Ooh. Bad image.

Maggie shuddered and put a hand to her mouth. She cried as the officers handled the body with respect and caring. A human being's life had been lost. Oh, no. Her numbness had worn off; pain and fear seeped into her awareness. She fought off panic. Leaning back in her glider, she prayed for this man who had been her enemy. Oh, Lord. He had a wife. Where was Jenny Sweeney, anyhow? Maggie wished she had taken time to develop a friendship with the sad, mousy woman.

As the officers brought their burden up to the sea wall, Ferguson and Jones returned and helped to lift the body up onto the grass. The detective bent over the body and surveyed it from head to toe. No visible wounds that Maggie could tell. "What's this?" he said. The others gathered to peer at the dead man's foot.

Maggie ran to fetch her binoculars. Sweeney's feet were bare, but on his right big toe he wore a blue bow—looked like sateen from this distance—about a quarter of an inch wide. What in the world…

Ferguson put his hands on his hips. "Do you suppose we're meant to believe this guy tied a ribbon on his own toe?"

The detective shook his head. "No way. But that bow symbolizes something to whoever tied it there."

"A blue bow. What could it mean?" Jones asked.

Ferguson puffed out his chest. "I used to get blue ribbons at horse shows. First prize."

Sheriff Dorsey snorted. "Maybe the killer thought this guy was a first prize...something."

A siren's call grew closer. An ambulance crossed the lawn between the buildings and came to a stop beside the sodden tarp with its morbid contents.

The detective turned to Ferguson and Jones. "What about that path in the grass?"

Jones took a step forward. "We followed the trail around the building and up to the stairwell."

"Did you take pictures?"

"Ferguson did."

Ferguson patted the deep pocket on his khakis to indicate the camera.

The ambulance attendants loaded the body, spoke a few soft words to the detective, and drove away. All four officers stood and watched the ambulance's departure.

The detective clasped his hands in front of his chest. "Let's go check out his condo. I wonder who has a key."

"I do," Maggie yelled down to them.

Four heads turned as one and stared up at her.

***

She met them at her front door with the keys. "Our condo president is away. She asked me to keep the keys to the units."

"Good morning, ma'am. I'm Detective Dorsey, and these are some of my officers." He indicated the rookies shifting from one foot to the other behind him. "Are you the lady who called us?"

"Yes. I'm Maggie Cartwright. Can I get you something to drink?"

"No, thank you, ma'am. This has all been a shock to you, I'm sure. Did you recognize the man?"

"Yes, he's Chuck Sweeney. He lives—lived—three doors down from me." She searched through the ring of keys to find Mr. Sweeney's. "I don't believe his wife is home." She removed the correct key from the ring and handed it to the detective. "Would you like to come in?"

"Not yet, ma'am. But I'd appreciate it if you would wait here for me."

"Yes, of course."

***

Maggie closed the door and pulled the rocking chair in her living room up close to the sliding glass doors facing the river beyond her patio. As she rocked, she focused on her breathing. The river now appeared calm and showed no evidence of a shocking death scene. Small waves lapped against the sea wall and created a soothing rhythm.

So much for an idyllic retirement. She wondered when the detective would return. He must be going over every inch of the deceased's condo with a magnifying glass. The way he assessed the river scene showed him to be observant. His piercing blue eyes wouldn't miss much. He suspected foul play and found a trail in the grass right away. What would he make of the blue bow? That surely was a strange touch. She shivered. Her rocker creaked in time to the river. Later, she would visit Jenny. What on earth would she say to her? 'Sorry about your ribbon-bedecked, cheating spouse's fatal flop in the river?' She stopped shuddering and got up to make a pot of tea.

A whirring and clawing from the bathroom startled her. Her cat shot out of the bathroom, missed careening into her by inches, and zoomed toward her bedroom. He trailed a long line of toilet paper between his teeth.

"Chaos! Not again." Maggie followed the scoundrel.

Two yellow eyes peered from just beneath the bed. The cat crept forward, toilet paper still hanging from his mouth, and swished his tail.

Maggie put her hands on her hips and entered the staring contest.

Chaos inched ever closer. Near Maggie's feet, he rolled over on his back and waited for a belly rub. Maggie complied. "You think you are the cleverest cat ever, don't you?"

The doorbell rang. Chaos leapt up in a flurry of black fur, dropped his prize, and darted back under the bed.

Through the smoked glass window pane beside her door, Maggie made out the tall, muscular figure of Detective Dorsey.

Maggie invited him in and offered him a cup of tea. This time he accepted, glancing around her condo.

"I see you have a cat," he said.

"More like a demon. He has a toilet paper fixation, amongst his many bad habits. Please make yourself at home."

She bustled around the kitchen making the tea and keeping one eye on him via the pass-through to the living room. He looked harmless enough in spite of his size. His expression betrayed nothing, invited no worries. He leaned back in her armchair and glanced toward the river. "Beautiful view here."

"Yes. It's very relaxing. Until this morning, that is."

She brought in a tray with tea, milk, and sugar and placed it on the table at his elbow.

He picked up the teapot and poured for them both. "Milk and sugar?"

"No, just milk, please." Ignoring toilet paper draped around one rocker, she pulled her rocking chair to face him and took the cup he offered. Both sipped in silence for a moment.

"Tell me about Mr. Sweeney," the detective said.

Maggie fought the urge to grimace and squirm. "I don't know what to say in a situation like this. He and I weren't close." She set her cup on the table and hoped he didn't notice the slight rattle caused by her shaking hands. She clasped her hands together and waited.

He leaned back farther in his chair. "People don't like to speak ill of the dead," he said. "But we need to know about his personality and habits in order to solve the crime."

Maggie looked up into his eyes and assumed what she hoped was an innocent expression. "Crime? Then it wasn't the alligator."

"No, I'm afraid not. Mr. Sweeney was killed in his condo and dragged into the river."

Maggie took a sharp intake of breath. "You know that already?"

"Yes. The murderer left a faint trail leading from the stairwell, around the condo, and to the river. But back to his personality. What was he like?"

Maggie fixed her eyes on his teacup. "Well…to tell you the truth…I don't know anybody who liked him."

"Why was that?" Detective Dorsey cocked his head slightly.

"He was the self-appointed condo commando." She met his eyes. "He made a habit of offending everyone about what he saw as the rules for condo living. People complained to the board about him, but he only seemed to get worse. Especially when he had been drinking, which was usually the case." She pushed a stray lock of hair behind her ear.

"Did you have any run-ins with him?"

Maggie looked at the floor. "Yes."

"When was the last time?"

She hesitated. "Yesterday afternoon, at the pool. He had a fit because I left the gate open while I retrieved a towel from my car. I was parked right in front of the pool."

"He sounds like a very up-tight man."

"You can say that again."

Detective Dorsey leaned forward and spoke in a gentle voice. "I'm glad you're telling me about this, Mrs. Cartwright, because two of your neighbors couldn't wait to report to me about overhearing you threaten to kill him yesterday. Are they right?"

Maggie blinked at him and drew a deep breath. "I think I did say something threating. He was just so exasperating… Oh, Lord. And now he's dead." She gaped at him and brought her hands to her mouth. His expressionless gaze bored through her.

"Exactly what did you say to him?"

Maggie sat up straighter. "Well, I may have told him if the bottle of suntan lotion I was carrying weighed half as much as his fat, ego-inflated head, I would swat him dead with it like the annoying insect he was." She looked at her hands, folded in her lap.

Detective Dorsey covered his mouth with one hand and cleared his throat. "And what was his response?"

"Oh, he went off spluttering and fuming toward the condos. Like most bullies, when you face them down, they turn tail."

"And you've had experience with bullies?"

Maggie stared at him. "I taught school for forty years. Of course I've dealt with bullies. And not all of them were in the administration." She rocked her chair and waited.

***

A crash in the bedroom startled Maggie. She stood. "That darn cat is at it again."

Detective Dorsey followed her into the room, where a large sewing basket lay upturned on the floor. Various skeins of embroidery thread, spools of sewing thread, crochet hooks, scraps of fabric, lengths of lace, and edging materials sprawled across the light oak floor and created a crazy collage of vibrant color.

"He's a modern artist," the detective said.

"He's a lunatic." Maggie bent to peer under the bed.

Chaos sidled out, wrapped in yellow yarn, red and green thread, and dust bunnies. He simpered up to the detective and rolled on his back. Detective Dorsey leaned over to pet him.

"What's this?" he asked. Looped around the cat's back legs and tail was a two-foot length of quarter-inch blue sateen ribbon. The lawman glanced at Maggie and then scratched the cat's belly with one hand while he unwound the ribbon with the other. The cat's loud purr ceased when the man held up the trophy. Chaos rolled to his feet, leapt for his ribbon, caught it between his paws, took it in his teeth, and darted back under the bed faster than the detective could react. Maggie and the detective peered under the bed. Ears pinned back, the bristling cat sat with his back to them, swishing his tail and guarding his prize. He growled when Maggie reached for him.

The detective surveyed the tangled mess on the floor. "Never mind, Ms. Cartwright. He left us a small piece here." He untangled a six-inch length of the same ribbon from the yarn and thread on the floor. Holding it up for Maggie to see, he asked, "May I keep this?"

"Of course," she replied.

Leaving Chaos with his swath of destruction, Maggie and the detective returned to their places in the living room.

Detective Dorsey broke the awkward silence. "Did you know that the victim wore a similar ribbon, tied in a bow, on his right big toe?" He regarded Maggie with a serious but patient expression.

Heat rose up Maggie's neck and to her cheeks. "Well…I watched from the balcony."

"Could you make out the ribbon from there?"

Maggie's face grew hotter. "I used my binoculars."

The detective restrained a smile. "You realize how this looks," he said. "You have the only extra key to the victim's condo; you threatened publicly to kill him yesterday; you have ribbon similar to if not the same as the ribbon found on the body. Any chance you have an alibi for last night?"

Maggie took a sharp breath. She looked away from the officer and paused to calm herself. "No… I was here alone. I went to bed about nine o'clock. By seven a. m. I was out by the river in my lawn chair."

"Did anyone call you last night? Did you send any e-mails or text messages?"

"I'm afraid not."

"I'm so sorry to ask you this, but I have to." He paused. "Did you kill Mr. Sweeney?"

Maggie gasped. "Of course not. I didn't like the man, but I'm not alone in that. Mr. Sweeney offended everyone indiscriminately. You shouldn't have any trouble discovering that."

"Do you know anything about his relationship with his wife?"

Maggie hoped he didn't notice her hesitation. "Not much. She keeps to herself. Seems timid. A few times I've seen her at the mail boxes with bruises on her face and arms. Mr. Sweeney was known to drink."

"Do you have any hunch about who killed him?"

"No. There's no one at the condos I would suspect of murder. Could he have been involved in some shady business outside of here?"

"It's too soon to know that." The detective rose to leave. "Thank you for the tea and for your frankness, Ms. Cartwright. Do you have any plans to leave the country?"

"None."

"Good. I need to ask you to keep yourself available until we clear this matter up." He rose from his chair and placed the condo keys on the end table.

Maggie showed him to the door and walked in a daze to her chair. Chaos strolled to her, dragging his blue ribbon. He dropped it at her feet.

"Chaos, you hellcat, you just framed me for murder, and I may be going to jail." She shook her head, rose from her chair, and stooped to pick up the scattered toilet paper and sewing materials.

***

With her condo tidy once again and Chaos curled up on her bed asleep, Maggie decided to visit the Sweeney condo. She needed to be proactive if she were to avoid a murder arrest. She stuck a clean pair of gloves in her apron pocket and paused outside her door. The late afternoon sun warmed her face and arms. The coast was clear. She walked to the condo two doors down, stooped under the yellow crime tape, and entered as though she had every right in the world to be there. She stopped in the small entryway and surveyed the scene. The condo had the same layout as hers. Minimally furnished and basically tidy, it provided no obvious clues. She sniffed the air. Was that a faint aroma of whiskey? No surprise there. Chuck Sweeney nearly always smelled of whiskey.

A pair of scuffed leather shoes, brown, near the door caught her attention. Obviously the victim's. Somebody placed his shoes neatly by the door as if in readiness to slip on before leaving the house. Come to think of it, he probably left them there himself. Lots of people kick their shoes off at the door when they enter the house. Control freak that he was, he probably did that, too. He was found barefoot. So where were his socks?

She poked around the bedroom walk-in closet and found a clothes hamper. On top were a pair of men's white socks. Hmm. So he came in, took off his shoes and socks, and what? Waited to be killed?

His bed was made. Hmm. No comforter or bedspread. Just drab beige sheets. The dull tan bedroom revealed nothing of interest except for its Spartan plainness. The man could have been a monk if he didn't have the personality of a cornered weasel. No touch of warmth or romance in this home. She shook her head and turned to the living room.

Now where would an autocrat sit? Ah yes. A big overstuffed recliner sat angled in a corner with a view to the river. The boss's chair. On the table beside it were a plain round coaster, a small lamp, and a stack of books. *The History of the Ku Klux Klan*, *Mein Kampf*, and *The Nazis and the Occult*. Tsk, tsk. She doubted if the victim had the brains to read, but she wasn't surprised at the subject matter. The last one sounded interesting…

She gave the room a thorough look without disturbing anything. No sign of Jenny's personality anywhere. No pictures, no artwork. Plain white walls. Brown couch, plain wooden coffee table without knick-knacks of any kind. What a sterile, unappealing environment. She should turn Chaos loose up here for a few hours, bring some life to the place.

The kitchen was clean. Nothing on the counter except a pitcher and a glass, both turned upside down to drain on a dish towel. Dry now, of course.

A key turned in the lock. Maggie ripped off her gloves, stuffed them in her pocket, and swiveled her head frantically in search of somewhere to hide. No use. She was caught.

A frail woman with long, limp, graying brown hair closed the door behind her, headed down the hall, and stopped short at the sight of Maggie.

Maggie straightened her back and squared her shoulders. "Jenny, you're home."

***

The woman burst into tears. Maggie ran to her and enveloped her in a hug. "There, there now. You've had a horrible shock. Come sit down, and I'll make you some tea."

Mrs. Sweeney allowed Maggie to lead her to the living room. "Not there." She indicated her husband's chair. "Chuck never allows me to…" Still crying, she put her hands to her face. Maggie guided her to the couch.

The widow wept quietly while Maggie prepared tea and thanked God for the distraction it created.

Accepting the hot, sweet liquid, Mrs. Sweeney took a sip and asked, "What are you doing here anyway?"

"I was the one who called the sheriff. It occurred to me that I ought to come here and make sure that you wouldn't walk in to any unpleasant surprises. It seems all is in order."

Mrs. Sweeney smiled through her tears. "That's a surprise in itself. Chuck normally didn't even pick up his socks." A new torrent of tears followed.

"The detective asked me a lot of questions. He told me not to leave the country. Jenny, I hope you know that in spite of our differences, I would never in a million years even consider harming your husband." Maggie leaned toward her and met her eyes.

"Oh, I know you wouldn't. I'm just so shaken and afraid. I don't think I can stay here anymore."

"Will you be able to stay with your sister?"

"Yes. That's where I've been. I needed to get away from…I needed to get away for a while. I'll go back to her house after the detective interviews me." She trembled.

"He's a very pleasant man. You'll be comfortable enough talking to him."

Jenny stared at her. "I don't think so. I wish it would all just go away. Could you stay with me until he comes?"

"Of course I will. Can I get you something to eat? Toast and jelly?"

"No, thank you. I don't think I could eat."

The widow lay curled on her couch and sniffed from time to time. Maggie sat at her feet and waited.

When the doorbell announced the detective's arrival, Maggie opened the door. He looked at her in surprise. "Well, Ms. Cartwright. Fancy meeting you here."

"Jenny asked me to wait with her. I'll be on my way now." Over her shoulder she called, "Jenny, let me know if you need anything." She felt the detective's eyes following her as she walked down the hall toward her own condo.

***

Maggie passed her own unit and continued to the stairwell. Time to visit Naomi.

Naomi met her at the door and hurried her inside. "I saw the detective leave your condo. Did you go and blab to him about me and Chuck?"

"Good evening to you, too. May I have a seat?"

"Oh, all right." She showed Maggie to an overstuffed chair in the living room. "Do you want tea?"

"Lord, don't even mention it to me. I've been drinking tea all day. I came to reassure you—your secrets are safe with me. Did you know Old Greensides is innocent?"

"Yes, I heard. Who could have killed Chuck?" She took a seat on a footstool across from Maggie.

"Most any of us, I imagine. But who do you suspect?"

"I have no idea, but…"

"Yes?"

"It's just that I'm pretty sure I'm not—wasn't—the only other woman in Chuck's life." Bitterness tinged her words.

"How do you know?"

"I went through the bastard's pockets one night." She glared. "I found a little black book with several other numbers in it. All listings were for females. When I confronted him, he laughed and said the numbers were from before my time. So why was he still carrying them around? I thought about calling the other women, but I felt humiliated enough already."

"Humiliated enough to kill him?"

"Be serious."

"Naomi, what on earth did you see in that man?"

She sighed. "Maggie, if you tell another soul, you'll be the next body in the river."

Maggie nodded.

"I can't make ends meet on my salary. Chuck helped with my bills."

The women sat in silence.

When Maggie spoke, her tone was ominous. "Seems like you have motive, Naomi. Be prepared. Detective Dorsey is nobody's fool, and he's already put me through the third degree."

***

At midnight Maggie walked around to the side of the building where the detective had found the trail in the grass. The far stairwell opened onto a short sidewalk at the end of the building. The side of the condo where Maggie stood faced a county park. Dark and uninhabited at night. No reason for anyone to pass through here. She looked up. No windows on this side. Hauling a body down stairs and through this narrow side yard wouldn't likely attract attention in the middle of the night. Even Sal, the condo queen of nosiness, would be asleep. Maggie stood still and listened. Only the river, lapping against the sea wall, broke the silence. The body must have made a splash when it hit the water, but the condo dwellers were used to dolphins, manatees, birds, and mullet thrashing and breeching. During manatee mating season, the noise was incredible.

A beam of light hit Maggie's back. She spun. The flashlight blinded her. She shielded her eyes and froze.

"Well, well, well. Re-enacting the crime. I wondered who might return to the scene." Detective Dorsey's voice startled, then infuriated Maggie.

"Don't you ever sleep?" she snarled.

"Looks like you're awake, too. What are you doing here?"

"Exactly like you said. Re-enacting the crime. Getting an idea of how easy it would be to go unnoticed while lugging a body to the river."

The detective shone his light on the ground from her to the river. "Nothing to it, I'd guess. But as a resident, you'd already know that."

"Look, Detective. Your suspicion of me has given me a heightened interest in understanding this case. Somebody has to solve it. If I leave it to you, you'll clap me behind bars before I can figure it out."

He ignored the insult. "Since you're up, do you mind if I have another look in your unit?"

"Be my guest. What are you looking for? Another body or two?"

"Anti-freeze. The coroner said that was the poison used to kill Mr. Sweeney."

"You're wasting your time. I haven't had anti-freeze in my house as long as I've lived here." She trudged back to the condo ahead of him.

Back in her unit, she stood with her hands on her hips while he poked around her hall closet and the cabinet under her sink.

"This is silly, you know," she said. "Anyone using antifreeze would have thrown the container away. Have you looked in our dumpster?"

He straightened to his full height and looked down at her. "Let's look now." He turned and led the way.

When the detective lifted the lid, an overwhelming stench of rotten meat combined with the stink of other sunbaked detritus hit Maggie's nose and pushed her back. A couple of cockroaches scurried down the front of the dirty green bin.

Thank God, the search was easy. On top of the trash lay a container of anti-freeze, more than half full. Dorsey looked at Maggie, who shot him an I-told-you-so smirk. He used a discarded newspaper to lift the item from the trash.

"Unless the killer was an idiot, you won't find any prints on that thing," Maggie said.

"Well, well, Mrs. Cartwright. If you turn out to be innocent, I may have a place for you on the force."

"No, thanks. All I want is to enjoy my retirement in peace."

"One thing's for sure. Chuck Sweeney won't be disrupting your tranquility anymore."

Maggie glared at him, turned, and stomped off to her condo.

***

Drip, splat, drip, splat—dripping water sounds greeted Maggie as she came through her front door. In the bathroom, Chaos sat at the side of the sink watching the water drip and swatting drops onto the mirror. He glanced briefly at Maggie before going back to work. Water trickled down the mirror in artistic rivulets.

"Hey, I'll bring you some Windex and a rag if you really want to clean that mirror." She left the cat with the dripping faucet and made herself comfortable in her rocker. Damn that infuriating cop, anyway. He was going to arrest her any time now if she didn't solve this murder. She rocked harder. The chair creaked from released anger. Chaos must have sensed her mood. He tore out of the bathroom and careened around the walls with every hair on end. "Go, cat, go. I may just join you."

Chaos came to an abrupt stop across the room from her. He arched his back like a Halloween cat, burred his tail, and bunny-hopped sideways toward her.

"Really, Chaos? You've already framed me for murder. Do you think this little scene will impress me?" She tsked and shook her head at the crazed feline. Chaos stopped and sat at her feet. He switched his tail and narrowed his yellow devil eyes.

Maggie sighed, rose from her chair, and walked to the kitchen, where she retrieved a large paper bag from under the sink. She brought it to Chaos. "Here. Try some of your deconstructive art on this."

The cat pounced into the bag and rolled with it across the carpet until he hit the far wall. Maggie shook her head again. Nuts. He was totally nuts. Stillness ensued while she returned to her seat. Had he knocked himself out? "Good. Take a nap in there while I get my thoughts straight."

She rocked, quietly this time, and reviewed her options. Ribbon. The corpse's damning blue ribbon that seemed to be a match for the one Chaos had given the detective on a silver platter. Who else might have ribbon like that? She rocked and thought. Nothing to be done tonight. She may as well get a good night's sleep and tackle this problem in the morning. She wasn't going to jail without a fight.

She stood, stretched, and headed for her bedroom. At the door, she turned. "Chaos, crazy I can tolerate. But disloyalty? Give me one good reason I shouldn't take you straight to the pound."

Scratch, rip, shred came from the bag. Chaos had begun his art project.

***

The next morning Maggie awoke early. She had to. She was being smothered. Twenty pounds of Chaos lay across her face and neck. She heaved his dead weight off to one side, where he flopped like an oversized beanbag. "You're out to get me one way or another, aren't you?"

The cat beat his tail on the bedspread and pinned his ears back.

Maggie slapped cat hair from her face and peeled back the bed covers. "Are you ready for breakfast?"

Like a shot out of a cannon, Chaos transported himself to the kitchen. He yowled his impatience and paced in front of the cat food cabinet.

"Okay, okay, I'm coming." Maggie scuffed into the kitchen in her worn slippers and opened the cabinet. The traitorous pet wound in and out of her legs and meowed as though he hadn't had a good meal in weeks.

"How about chicken this morning?"

The volume increased.

"I'll take that as a yes." She opened a can of flaked white chicken and forked it out into Chaos's ceramic dish. The one with the fish etched on the inside bottom. She sprinkled some dry kibble on the chicken and mixed it. When she placed the dish on Chaos's placemat—the one with cute kitties, not demons, on it—the egocentric beast tore into his breakfast like the Coliseum lions must have torn into the Christians.

After changing the litter box and mixing the fresh litter with baking soda, Maggie washed up, collected her purse, and headed for the front door. She looked at her cat. "Bye, Chaos. And no more colluding with that evil detective while I'm gone."

Ignoring her, Chaos crunched and smacked his lips as he inhaled his breakfast.

"I'll miss you, too," said Maggie.

***

Wal-mart, Joanne's, Michael's, and Hobby Lobby. Those were the obvious starting places to search for ribbon.

She stood at the ribbon aisle in Michael's and sighed. Her back ached. She dragged her tired feet up and down aisles. Polka dot satin, polyester ric rac, head band elastic, mouse tail cord, organza, velvet, velveteen, and lace—no end to the types, colors, and prints of ribbon. But not a trace of what she was looking for. Maggie turned the ribbon spool—the one she had found at home—over in her hands. Its white cardboard had yellowed with time, but she could still clearly read "cobalt blue sateen ribbon" on the label. A short length still hung from the spool where the end was taped. She couldn't remember where or when or for what she had bought it. She wouldn't be surprised if it were twenty years or more old. She sighed and slid the spool back in her purse.

Approaching the oldest worker in the fabrics section, Maggie asked, "Do you remember sateen ribbons?"

The chubby, graying store clerk nodded as she rolled pink print flannel back on its bolt. "Oh, sure. But I haven't seen any in a long time. Now it's nearly all polyester and some satin."

Maggie smiled. "Yes, that's what I'm discovering. I'm trying to match some ribbon that's clearly outdated. I can't even find the exact shade of blue." She took the spool out and handed it to the clerk, who turned it over and read the label.

"I haven't seen this in ages. I'm sorry, but I'm afraid we can't get the same ribbon for you. Have you tried flea markets or garage sales?" She handed the spool back with a frown.

Maggie placed the ribbon in her purse. "That's an idea. Thank you for your help."

It was the same story at all the other stores. Maggie was no closer to a solution.

As she walked back to her car after the last store, she hoped the killer wasn't a collector of old ribbon. Or someone who stole her ribbon in order to frame her. She shuddered. Maybe she would catch a break, and the sheriff's department would discover that her ribbon was not the same as that on the corpse's toe.

Back at her unit, she searched the internet for "sateen" and "satin" while Chaos sat on her desk, supervised, and occasionally swatted at images on the monitor.

"Listen, Chaos. This is interesting. Sateen is cotton, sometimes soaked in acid, woven with a special weave pattern—four threads up and one down. This gives the fabric luster but also weakens it. Satin, on the other hand, is traditionally silk with a one up, one down weave pattern."

Maggie leaned back in her chair and rubbed her chin. "Obviously, with the advent of polyester, which could be produced to shine, manufacturers no longer needed to put the now precious cotton through a costly process to make sateen. Hmm…"

She printed the information and put it in her desk drawer along with the spool and ribbon sample. She'd share the printouts with the detective, but she'd be damned if he'd get his hands on her last ribbon sample. Let him use what he already took and figure it out for himself.

Tired from her morning errands, she rose, stretched, and yawned. Was a short nap in order?

With her attention turned from her task, the eerie quiet of the condo disturbed her. Where was that devil cat? A thorough search of the unit turned him up at last. He slept soundly in a nest he had fashioned out of her sweaters on the top shelf of her closet. Garments deemed unsuitable for his majesty had been banished from the shelf to the closet floor, where they lay in rejected disarray.

Shaking her head, Maggie tiptoed from the room to let the sleeping cat lie.

Dozing in her rocking chair, Maggie shot straight up when the doorbell rang. What now? Good, Lord. Was that pesky detective back again? She looked around her unit. No use trying to hide. Her car was parked out front. She sighed and lumbered to the door. Maybe she would get more rest in prison.

Sal Cameron blew into the condo like a whirlwind. Her perfectly styled and sprayed blond hair and precise makeup did little to mask her basic unattractiveness and heavy girth. "Gosh almighty,

Mags, aren't you afraid about this murder right here in our building? Do you mind if I sit down?" She wheezed her way to the recliner without waiting for a reply.

"Hello, Sal. Come on in. Can I get you something to drink?"

"You wouldn't have any ginger tea, would you? I declare, my stomach has been giving me fits ever since I heard about this tragedy." She leaned back and fanned her face with her hands.

While Maggie made the tea, Sal provided a running commentary. "You know that Chuck Sweeney was an alcoholic skirt-chaser, don't you? I wouldn't be surprised if he hit on you. I know my Donald wouldn't let me anywhere near him. Any number of women could have had a grudge against him. Can you hear me, Mags?" She leaned forward to peer at Maggie through the pass-through.

Maggie winced at the nickname. "Yes, I hear you." She poured boiling water over the tea bags.

"Well, I know who I would pick for the murderer. But, really, I have two theories." She leaned back, reclined the chair, and straightened her expensive skirt.

Maggie entered with the tea on a tray and placed it on the table near Sal. "What a lovely outfit."

"Oh, this old thing. I bought a few clothes three months ago for our Switzerland trip. We're going to Peru next month, so I really need to shop for different styles."

"Were you home when the body was found?" Maggie took her place in her rocker and tried to sound casual.

"Oh, no." Sal's voice conveyed a touch of regret. "We were on our way back from Australia. I only heard about it this morning."

"You said you had two theories." Maggie knew wild horses couldn't keep Sal from spilling everything she thought or imagined, but coaxing Sal along might get rid of her sooner.

"Yes. Didn't you have your air conditioner replaced last month?"

Maggie rocked slowly. Even with a marathon travel schedule, Sal never missed anything that happened in the condos. If she had been home when the murder occurred, Sal would have known it before the body hit the water. "Why, yes, I did."

Sal harrumphed. "Well, Mags, you do know that those service people can get into our condos when they go onto the roof, don't you? When I saw the van outside the first time, I left you a card from the air conditioning company I trust. Who knows what those cut-rate persons you hired are capable of?" She smirked.

Maggie stared at her. "Are you suggesting that my air conditioning installer entered Chuck Sweeney's condo *from the roof somehow* and killed him?"

"Why not? Chuck could have been seeing his wife."

"No, put that theory from your mind. I trust my air conditioner guy completely. I've known him a long time. I taught his brother." Maggie shook her head and rose. "More tea?"

"If it isn't too much trouble." Sal extended her cup.

On her way to the kitchen, Maggie asked over her shoulder, "And what is your second theory?" She glanced at Sal via the pass-through.

Sal rubbed her hands together in apparent enjoyment. Her crimson manicured nails reflected the light like rubies. "Three weeks ago, before our

Australian trip, you know, Chuck and that woman downstairs, Naomi, had the most awful fight. Of course I didn't want to listen, but they were too loud to avoid. I admit I was outraged because such common behavior only reduces the tone of our community and hurts all of us."

Maggie handed the refilled teacup to her. Sal took a sip.

"What did you do?" asked Maggie.

"I hesitated to call the police because police presence can brand a place as low class faster than the poor behavior of my neighbors, so I just waited it out."

Maggie stifled a sigh. Sal was going to drag out her delicious news as long as she could. "Did you hear what they were fighting about?"

"I heard everything. Naomi attacked Chuck because she had found his little black book of other women's numbers. At first, Chuck tried to placate her, but at the end, he was screaming louder than she was. He said, 'Naomi, we're through. You were fun for a while, but now you're too much of a nuisance'." Sal stared into her teacup as if she were reading the leaves.

"And what did Naomi say to that?"

Sal grinned. "She told him she ought to kill him for using her and tossing her aside. Then she slammed his door behind her and stomped down the stairs."

"Have you told any of this to the police?"

Sal looked up from her cup. "No. Do you think I should? I imagine they'll come calling when they realize we're home."

Maggie rubbed her chin and rocked. "That's a hard call. Naomi's our neighbor. In the heat of the moment, people threaten to kill others more often than is good for them. On the other hand, the man is dead. Maybe you'd better cooperate with the investigation and tell the truth if they call on you."

"Think so, Mags?" Sal set her empty cup down and studied her immaculate fingernails. She glanced around the condo. "You know, I have a great interior decorator I can recommend to you."

Maggie wondered how in the world she could get rid of the woman.

As if he had read her mind (he probably did), Chaos sailed into the room and landed upside down on Sal's lap where he kneaded all four paws in the air and uttered unearthly growls.

Frozen with shock, Sal stared in horror at the berserk animal. Maggie covered her mouth to hide a grin.

Sal leapt to her feet, wobbled on her Jimmy Choo heels, brushed cat fur from her Chanel skirt, and shrieked, "Mags! I told you to get rid of that insane beast."

***

After ushering an indignant Sal out the door, Maggie patted Chaos, who rubbed against her shins and wove in and out of her legs. He purred and arched his back as if to proclaim what a fine job he had done in ridding the house of obnoxious intruders, like undesirables who butted in with the nerve to interrupt his nap in the closet.

"Chaos, I'm leaving you in charge here. Well, I guess you always are in charge, aren't you? Anyway, I'm going out for a while. Hold down the fort." Maggie placed her hands on her hips and regarded the cat, who blinked his slanty eyes at her and sat at her feet with his tail wrapped around his paws. The picture of innocence. "Harumph. Who do you think you're fooling?" Maggie asked.

She collected her purse and headed for her car, an aging Toyota convertible. Buckling the seatbelt, she chuckled about the time she discouraged Sal from begging rides to the store. With her haughty neighbor seated smugly in the passenger seat, Maggie put the top down and drove ninety miles an hour up I-95. Sal's plastered-in-place helmet hairdo, shellacked hard enough to resist hurricane winds, got a little ruffled that day. She hadn't asked for a ride since then. Maggie inhaled deeply. She doubted that Sal would ever be involved in anything as messy as murder.

Maggie touched her own unruly hair and wondered when she had last combed it. Didn't matter, anyway. With or without combing, her chronically bed-headed hair stuck out in all directions. She sighed. She'd have to cede the grooming award to Sal. Anyway, other people's unkempt hair would be the last thing on Chuck's widow's mind.

The drive to Jenny Sweeney's sister's house in Orlando was pleasant enough. Little eastbound traffic at this time of day. On the outskirts of town, Maggie stopped to call Jenny's sister, Mary. A tentative female voice answered on the first ring.

"Mary? Maggie Cartwright here. I'm Jenny's neighbor. I'm in east Orlando, and I wondered if I might come by for a short visit."

"Oh. We met once when I was at Jenny's. Sure. Come by. Jenny is out walking, but she should be back any time now."

Maggie stopped at Publix to buy two large pans of food--one of chicken tenders and one of macaroni and cheese. She followed Mary's directions to the shady suburban street with deep green lawns and modest, well-kept houses. Mary's lawn was punctuated with flower beds. Yellow lilies complemented the pale yellow house. Lush green ferns formed a backdrop for marigolds, butter-colored roses, and daisies. The roses exuded the vigor of persistent care.

Mary opened the door.

"What lovely flowers you have," Maggie said.

Mary smiled. "Thank you. Gardening is a hobby of mine." She stood aside and motioned Maggie into an immaculate blue and yellow sitting room.

Maggie placed the food on the table in the adjoining kitchen and sank into an overstuffed arm chair. She sighed with pleasure.

"Thank you so much for coming, and for the food. What would you like to drink?" Mary asked.

"It was a warm drive. A glass of cold water would be perfect."

While Mary fetched the water, Maggie noted the contrast of the cheerful room and the aura of sadness emanating from Mary's gait, voice, and facial expression. Here was a woman whose world had been shaken. When she met Mary, Maggie had formed the impression of a gentle, timid woman, retiring and undemanding. Like Jenny, in fact, tall and thin, but blonder. Almost twin-like in the similarity of their personalities.

Mary returned with ice water and handed a glass to Maggie. She sat in an occasional chair opposite Maggie and placed her glass on the coffee table between them.

"How are you holding up?" Maggie asked.

Mary breathed deeply. "I don't know what to think or feel. I begged Jenny to leave Chuck for years, but she wouldn't listen. She blamed herself for the bruises he gave her, or blamed the Jim Beam he drank by the gallon. It was hard to watch her suffer…But then to have this happen, for Chuck to be murdered…now, it's strange…" She wrung her hands in her lap and stared at the wall behind Maggie. "I don't know whether to feel relief or grief."

"I'm sure you must feel some of both."

"Yes, well, but I had trouble sleeping before this. Hormonal changes, you know. I have been taking a sleeping medication for several weeks. It helps, but I'd like to be able to discontinue it. Chuck's death is a setback in that way, too."

"Give it time. At least now you won't have to worry about Jenny's victimization at the hands of an abusive husband. His being dead doesn't change what he was, but it stops the wrong he was doing." Maggie set her glass down with a thump. "I think it's okay to take comfort in that."

Mary stared wide-eyed at her. "Oh." She looked away. "Since you put it that way…I think you're right." She met Maggie's eyes.

The door opened. Both women turned their heads. Jenny entered and stopped when she caught sight of Maggie. "Oh, Maggie. How kind of you to visit." Her voice signaled fatigue and weakness. She walked into the room and took a chair beside her sister. Pain, defeat, or grief deepened the lines in her haggard face.

"Have you been able to eat, Jenny?" Maggie frowned with concern.

"I haven't had much appetite, and my stomach refuses most everything." Jenny sighed.

"Is there anything I can do for you? I brought chicken tenders and macaroni, but would you like some chicken and dumplings? That's one comfort food I know how to make." Maggie smiled.

"You're very kind, but right now I can barely stand the thought of food. Maybe later when my body adjusts. I never imagined how hard this could be…"

"Of course. But you'll get better with time. I'm glad you have Mary."

Jenny glanced at her sister, who sat with her hands folded in her lap. "Yes. Staying here with her is a great consolation. I don't know what I'd do without her." She smiled weakly at her sister.

Maggie waited for Jenny to fill the silence.

"The saddest part is that Chuck really was getting better. I always hoped and prayed he'd quit drinking. His actions weren't his fault. I have his friend Jim Beam to thank for that. He'd cut back on his drinking, and I had more hope for my marriage than I'd had in ten years…" She gazed wistfully into the distance and wiped a tear away with the back of her hand. Mary got up and found a box of tissues. She handed the box to Jenny.

"And then he had a setback?" Maggie asked.

"Yes. His boss at the realty office accused him of sexually harassing the female workers and fired him. Chuck came across as tough to anyone who didn't know him like I did, but he wasn't strong enough to handle losing his job." She sniffed and dabbed her eyes.

"You must've been very disappointed after having such hope."

Jenny looked at her feet. "Yes…it was a blow for me."

Maggie straightened her back. "Did you tell the investigators about Chuck's firing?"

"Oh yes. They wanted to know everything I knew about who might have had a grudge against Chuck."

Maggie sighed and bit her lip. That must have been a long list unless Jenny was in complete denial. "I am their chief suspect, I believe, because of the spat I had with Chuck at the pool."

Jenny looked up quickly, her eyes wide. "Oh, surely not."

"I'm afraid so. But this isn't about me. I won't keep you any longer, Jenny, but please call me if you want that chicken dinner or if there's anything else I can do for you and Mary. Even if you just want to talk." She rose and headed for the door. The sisters walked her to the door.

"Thank you for coming," they said in unison.

***

On the way back, Maggie mused about what she had learned. Mary and Jenny had clear alibis for each other unless Mary's use of sleeping medication made it possible for Jenny to leave at night undetected. Was timid Jenny capable of sneaking back to her condo at night, catching Chuck in some vile act, and killing him? That scenario was hard to imagine. Mary's distress seemed genuine, as did Jenny's. Were they both guilty—lying and covering for each other? If so, they had left no useful evidence. Maggie shook her head. This trip had been unproductive.

Back home, Maggie set her purse on the kitchen counter and looked around for Chaos. The gold sheer curtains framing her glass doors caught her eye. What was different about them?

"Oh, no," she exclaimed. "Chaos, do you like this fringed look better?" The curtains hung in ragged shreds from about two and a half feet off the floor. "PETA says that declawing is inhumane, but you're pushing the limits. Shredding my curtains is surely a form of elder abuse."

The self-satisfied rogue sauntered in from the bedroom, yawned, stretched, meowed a hello, and rubbed first against his unique window treatment and then against Maggie's legs.

Maggie's irritation evaporated. "Well, Chaos, there's no accounting for tastes. Maybe you're right. How about some dinner?"

Tail held high, he beat her to the kitchen.

***

When the doorbell rang the next morning, Chaos yowled and paced in front of the door until Maggie opened it to Detective Dorsey. He stooped to pet the cat, who purred and rubbed against his legs. "Hey, there, Chaos. At least one of you is happy to see me." He produced a catnip mouse from his pants pocket and held it by the tail. Chaos stretched his long body upward with both front paws extended and snagged the toy. Then he scurried off to hide it under the bed.

"Tea?" Maggie asked.

"If you don't mind."

She showed the detective to the chair he sat in before and left to prepare the tea. She looked at him through the opening to the kitchen. "Do you always bribe your informants?"

The detective laughed. "No. Chaos is special. Besides, the mouse was more of a reward. A bribe is paying somebody to do something wrong."

Maggie brought the tea and set the tray at the detective's elbow.

He poured them each a cup. They sat in silence and sipped the soothing beverage for a few minutes.

Maggie put her cup down. "Any progress?"

Detective Dorsey sighed. "Some. First, Mr. Sweeney's workplace is a wash for suspects. The three women and the boss, Mr. Evans, all have strong alibis for the time of the murder." He paused. "So our field of suspects is narrowing." He gazed at Maggie.

"I...I see." She crossed her arms and clutched her shoulders. "You said 'first'. Is there more?"

"Oh, just the ribbon. The lab report says the ribbon on the deceased's toe is a match for the sample from your condo."

Maggie inhaled deeply and stared at him. "But…but…that can't be. That ribbon hasn't been sold around here in years."

"How did you know that?"

"I searched all of the local craft stores and researched satin and sateen on the internet." She rose to retrieve the copies she had made and attached to the kitchen bulletin board. "Here you are." She presented the papers to the detective. "The store clerk told me that flea markets and garage sales were the best bets for finding this particular ribbon." She sat at the edge of her chair and waited, barely breathing.

He skimmed the printouts and frowned for what seemed to Maggie like an eternity. "You've been very busy, not to mention resourceful." He looked up from his reading and met her eyes. "Of course it's possible that the ribbon on Mr. Sweeney's toe was obtained elsewhere. But you must realize the likelihood seems remote."

Maggie took a deep breath. "Certainly I understand that. Tell me, Detective. Are books and writing materials provided in prison?"

Surprise flashed across his face. "Now, wait a minute. Let's not go there…just yet. There are a few more avenues of inquiry."

Chaos staggered in from the bedroom and flopped at Detective Dorsey's feet. He wallowed on his back, purred like a lawnmower, and pulled at the man's shoestrings until he had them both untied. Then he chewed on the ends.

Maggie finally spoke. "If I go to jail, Detective, you have to take this cat."

***

At a loss as to what she could do next to solve the murder, Maggie decided to focus on a problem she could do something about. She drove to Pet Co and examined the choices for scratching posts for cats. She settled on a deluxe model about five feet tall with several levels covered in carpet. Thick ropes and nets with toys attached festooned the elaborate apparatus. Boxes for hiding and holes for extending mischievous paws added to the feline attractions. Surely Chaos would leave her curtains and furniture alone with such a perfect playground available.

Two muscular store clerks loaded her purchase into the back seat of her convertible. Maggie drove cautiously along the strip mall until the liquor store caught her eye. A glass of wine would be nice. She pulled into the closest parking space and entered the store. She selected a Florida wine, Lake Ridge's Southern Red, and approached the cashier. There by the counter sat a display of Jim Beam whiskey. Maggie caught her breath. Advertising a brand anniversary, each bottle was adorned with a small blue bow. She touched a ribbon and turned it over in her hand. Yes. It looked like ribbon the detective had taken from her condo. She added a beribboned bottle to her wine purchase. What a surprise she would have for Detective Dorsey on his next visit. She smiled and thanked the cashier.

At home she found a couple of teenaged boys smoking in the parking lot.

"Hey, guys. I'll pay you ten dollars apiece to help me put this scratching post in my second floor condo."

They exchanged looks and walked toward Maggie's car. "That's no scratching post," said one. "It's a cat palace."

"Let's hope it keeps my monster off the furnishings," said Maggie.

Huffing and puffing, the young men installed the cat gymnasium in Maggie's living room. Chaos shot out of the bedroom, sailed straight to the top of his extravagant new toy, and struck a regal pose.

"Well, I'm glad you like it," Maggie said. "Now quit scratching up everything else in the house."

Chaos looked down at her and blinked his eyes.

Maggie took two crisp ten dollar bills from her purse and paid her helpers, who shuffled out the door.

She put the wine on its side in her cupboard and made a cup of ginger tea.

Considering her next move, she sat with her tea and rocked while Chaos beamed benevolently down at her. Should she call the detective? Probably. She studied the river, gray now, with little white-capped waves. Then she sighed and rose from the chair. "Chaos, you be good. I'm leaving you in charge again."

She headed for the door and down the steps to Naomi's apartment.

Naomi answered Maggie's knock with an air of exasperation. "Oh, it's you. Come on in." Her frown showed Maggie that her visit wasn't exactly welcome, but she led Maggie to a chair and plopped down opposite her. "What can I do for you?"

"I won't take up much of your time. You look frazzled. I just came by to see if you had any more news of the murder." Maggie relaxed with a conscious effort and made her voice as soothing as possible. Dealing with Naomi was a lot like dealing with Chaos. They both needed mega doses of relaxation therapy, if not psychiatric medication.

"I know I look like Hell. You don't have to remind me. I've been up since dawn cleaning this damn condo. I can't stay on top of it."

Maggie looked around at Naomi's gleaming condo. Spotless as usual. "You're a bit hard on yourself, you know. Everything looks fine."

Naomi's rigid posture gave a little. "Well, this place doesn't clean itself, I can tell you. Do you want tea or something to drink?"

Maggie knew the answer had better be no. "No, thank you. I won't be staying that long. I have a funny question for you. Do you know what Chuck Sweeney drank?"

Naomi eyed her for a long moment. "The bastard drank Jim Beam. Enough to float the *Kate Adams* from Memphis to New Orleans."

Maggie hoped her facial expression was blank. "Did you ever buy it for him?"

"Hell, no. Do you think I'm crazy? I may be an opportunist, but I'm no enabler. Why do you ask?"

Maggie inhaled deeply. "I've had another visit from Detective Dorsey. I'm just gathering all the information about Chuck I can before that suffocating arm of the law nails this murder on me."

Naomi settled back in her chair. "You've got to be kidding me."

"I wish I were. He seems to like me more and more as his chief suspect, so if you know anything that might clear me, I'd appreciate it. You knew the victim better than I did."

Naomi's expression was thoughtful. "Well, Maggie, if you killed the son of a bitch, the whole condo community owes you a favor. What kind of chocolate do you like?"

Maggie didn't miss a beat. "There's no such thing as bad chocolate. I'll put you on my jailhouse visitation list." She rose to leave. Naomi showed her to the door in silence.

***

Instead of returning to her condo, Maggie sighed and made her way to Sal's door. Might as well gather patience and face her one more time.

The door opened before Maggie could knock. Sal saw her coming. The woman must be psychic. Sal appeared, dressed like a Buckingham palace greeter. Not one lacquered hair dared move from its appointed place. Maggie ran a hand through her own raggedy mop. Had she combed her hair today? Will the prison grooming rules fit her style? She shook her head to clear it, took another deep breath, and entered Sal's ostentatious lair.

"You won't mind sitting in the kitchen, will you, Mags? I just cleaned my Corinthian leather living room furniture, and we're expecting an important visitor from the church hierarchy."

Maggie followed her to the bar stools at the kitchen island and wondered if the important visitor might be an exorcist. The elaborate gilt mirrors and extravagant brocade window treatments gave the place a jarring air. Didn't Sal realize she lives in Florida on a river?

Sal asked if she preferred a crystal glass of Perrier or tea in her Royal Doulton china. Maggie opted for the water, and Sal poured it over ice.

"Say, Mags, did I show you my letter from the President?"

"Yes, a few weeks ago. You should have it framed." She took a sip of fizzy water.

"Oh, we just keep it in a special drawer with all of our other priceless mementos." Sal shrugged. "I saw that detective at your place again. What's going on?"

Maggie hesitated. What the heck. Let her spread it all over the condo community. "What's going on, Sal, is that he is steadily building a case to arrest me for the murder of Chuck Sweeney."

Sal's mouth dropped open. She clutched her chest. "Oh, my. Oh, my," she murmured, trying unsuccessfully to hide her delight.

"So you can see I would appreciate any information you have that might help me clear my name. For instance, did you know what drink Mr. Sweeney preferred?"

"Everybody knows, Mags. He drank Jim Beam. I could tell his drink preference by his breath the day I moved in here. I said to Donald, 'Well, this guy ends my hopes for this neighborhood.' Sweeney is one of the reasons I questioned our judgement in moving here. We're not accustomed to a low class of people." She shuddered. "What you need, Mags, is a list of women he'd been seeing. Lucky for you, I just happen to have one. Something just told me to keep a journal on him. For our own security, you know. With that man bringing all kinds of disreputable women here, who knew what might happen? They could have broken in here to take our irreplaceable artwork and artifacts." She rose and rummaged through a drawer. "Between you and me, Mags, his death is good riddance to bad rubbish." She handed Maggie a small green velvet notebook. "This is for your eyes only."

Maggie turned the book over in her hands and opened it. The entries dated from three years prior to just a few weeks before Sweeney's death. "Why didn't you give this to the sheriff's department?"

Sal lifted her nose into the air and sniffed. "I don't like to encourage the police to hang around here. Police presence brings down the neighborhood. I'm only giving it to you in hopes you can solve this thing and put the whole sordid business behind us."

A huge imported cuckoo clock chimed the hour. Maggie rose to take her leave. Grateful to the expected important visitor for making her escape easier, she ambled back to her condo.

The distinct aroma of catnip struck her nose as she entered her home. Maggie stopped at the end of the small entryway and surveyed the scene. The catnip mouse had been gutted, its contents sprinkled on the living room floor. Gray feathers from a feather duster that had also been slain dotted the floor and the sofa. Down floated in the air. Shreds of a brown paper bag from the kitchen trailed into the bathroom, where the toilet paper lay in a mound on the floor. Chaos lay sleeping on his side on the top layer of his scratching post. His head lolled off of the platform.

Maggie put her hands on her hips. "Chaos, I should have talked to you about catnip when you were a kitten, before it was too late."

The cat snored.

***

Maggie awoke the next morning with two ideas swirling in her head. She stared at the ceiling and brushed Chaos's tail away from her face. One of the women she talked to had given her a clue. She would follow through on that later. The other idea she could check out right after breakfast.

She dressed quickly and fed her complaining cat, who, miffed at her inattention, sat with his back turned to her and refused to eat. "Sorry, Chaos. I have a lot on my mind this morning." She stooped to pet him absentmindedly until he relented and turned to his food.

"I hope it's not too early for those boys to be about," she said.

Leaving Chaos absorbed with his breakfast, she walked outside onto the front landing and searched the parking lot. Under their favorite tree stood the two youths she had paid to carry the cat palace into her condo. She waved to them. They looked at each other, stomped out their cigarettes, and walked across the parking lot and up to Maggie.

"Would you like to earn another ten dollars each?" she asked. "I need help with a little experiment."

"Sure," they answered together.

Maggie showed them into her condo and offered them a drink. They refused and looked at her with questioning eyes.

"This may sound crazy, but I'd like to see if I could drag one of you across my floor."

The boys looked at each other and shrugged.

"You go first, Jim," said one.

Jim lay on the carpet. "Do you want me on my stomach or on my back?"

"Let's try this with you on your back. Just raise your hands over your head, please."

Maggie took a deep breath and grasped Jim's hands. She pulled him several inches across the floor before letting go.

"This sure is hard," she said. She stood panting.

The other young man drawled, "Excuse me, ma'am. Not that I've had any experience in moving bodies, but you ain't gonna get anywhere that-a-way. Now if'n you rolled him onto a slick sheet, you could haul him a right smart easier."

Jim looked up from the floor at his companion. "Jesse, where on earth did you learn that?"

Jesse shuffled from one foot to the other and looked at the floor. "Well, in Kentucky I used to help my granpaw move hawg carcasses and such like that."

"Wait here, boys," said Maggie.

From her linen closet she retrieved a polyester bedspread. "Okay, Jesse, your turn."

She spread the bedspread on the floor, and Jesse took his place on it. This time Maggie pulled the bedspread across the floor with much less effort in spite of the fact that Chaos insisted on riding on Jesse's stomach.

"Thank you so much," she said. "You two have helped me answer an important question."

Jim and Jesse grinned and waited while Maggie retrieved her purse. She handed a ten dollar bill to each of them.

At the door, Jim turned and asked, "We're glad to help, ma'am, but do you mind telling us why you wanted to know how to move a body?"

"I could tell you," Maggie said. "But then I'd have to take you on an unscheduled bedspread slide."

The youths glanced at each other, pocketed their money, and hurried down the steps.

Maggie closed the door and smiled at Chaos, who was busily twanging the door stopper.

***

Pretty sure she already knew who the killer was, Maggie reluctantly tackled the next task. She opened the green notebook that Sal had given her, sighed, and, cell phone in hand, sat in her rocker.

Fifteen names. Fifteen women in three years. She guessed it could have been worse.

Taking a deep breath, Maggie called the first number. Disconnected. She had the same luck with the next two. She hoped these three women had moved on to better lives.

The fourth call was answered on the first ring by a soft female voice.

"Darlene Pinsky?"

"Yes?"

"My name is Maggie Cartwright. I'm calling to ask if you are aware that Chuck Sweeney was found dead in the river earlier this week."

"What? Chuck? Found dead?" A moment of silence on the line was followed by wails so loud that Maggie had to remove the phone from her ear.

Maggie listened to uncontrolled shrieking and crying for a few minutes.

Finally, Darlene caught her breath. "Wh…what happened? Are you sure? He can't be gone just like that." The wailing resumed.

"Listen, Darlene. I'm sorry to break this to you, but I'm Chuck's neighbor, and I thought you'd like to know."

Darlene sniffed loudly. "I-I talked to him only last week. He was finally going to leave his wife and marry me." She sobbed. "I don't know why I'm telling you this. I can't go on without him. What am I going to do?"

Deep gasps and an increasing tone of panic on the line alarmed Maggie. "Do you have any family, Darlene?"

"Y-yes."

The young woman's sobs and rapid breathing rumbled in Maggie's ear. Maggie held the phone farther away from her head.

"My mother lives in Orlando," Darlene said.

"You probably need to stay with her. This has obviously been a shock for you."

"How…how did he die?"

"The sheriff's department is investigating his death as a homicide. Do you know anyone who would want to kill him?"

"No, he was the most wonderful man in the world." Darlene's loud nasal voice hurt Maggie's unbelieving ears.

"How old are you, Darlene?"

"Twenty-five. But the age difference didn't matter. We were soul mates." A note of defiance accompanied the hysteria.

"Do you have a friend you could call to help you get to your mother's house?"

"Y-yes. No. But I can call my mom and she'll come over."

"Will you promise me you'll do that?"

"Y-yes. I want my mom," she wailed.

Maggie said goodbye, hung up, and shook her head. Oh, Lord Almighty. Her next call was to Detective Dorsey.

"Look," she said when he came to the phone. "I have a list of the recent women in Chuck Sweeney's life. I called one of them, and that was enough drama for me. I'll tell you all about it if you'll come over and take this damn notebook."

"I'll be right there."

***

Maggie showed Detective Dorsey in and made tea while Chaos purred like a Ferrari in his lap, rubbed his cheek against the detective's cheek, and head-butted him.

When they were settled with their tea, Detective Dorsey took the notebook and opened it. He smiled as Maggie told him about her conversation with Darlene.

"Believe it or not, I already have more than half of these names." He nodded toward the open notebook. I had similar experiences when I called Rhea, Lavender, and Cady. They all thought Chuck Sweeney hung the moon. All reported similar promises of marriage. So far, all of them have excellent alibis for the time of the murder." He pushed Chaos out of his face to take a sip of tea.

"If the condo residents learn of Chuck's prowess as a ladies' man, they may have more respect for him." Maggie rocked slowly and drank her tea.

"You know how it goes sometimes. You're no body till somebody kills you."

Maggie set her cup down. "That's not funny."

Chaos leaned over to examine the cup's contents and began kneading the detective's thighs with his claws.

"Ouch! Easy, there, buddy. I suppose you aren't going to tell me where you got the notebook."

"Oh, yes I will. Maybe it will make her mad enough to leave me alone. It was Sal. She took three years' worth of notes on the comings and goings at the Sweeney condo."

Detective Dorsey rolled his eyes.

"Between you and me, Detective, I don't think Chuck was killed by any of the women in this notebook." Maggie leaned back in her chair.

"Do you have an idea who did it?"

"Yes. I have a couple more things to check out. Then I'll report back to you."

"No way, Miss Marple. You're either doing a clever job of detracting attention from yourself, or you are getting ready to put yourself in danger. You tell me your theory and let me check it out."

"Oh, no. As much as I like you, Detective, I don't trust you not to slap me in the big house, or whatever you call it." She rose and picked up their teacups.

Dislodging Chaos from his lap, Detective Dorsey rose to his full height and looked down at Maggie with a stern face. "This is a murder investigation. I hope you are not suppressing any evidence. That would be a serious crime."

Maggie met his eyes. "I'm well aware of that."

Chaos followed them to the door as Maggie showed the disgruntled detective out.

***

Maggie walked in the park beside the condos. Two children played on the swings while their mother read a book on a nearby bench. A toddler sat in the sandbox eating sand with both fists. The river lapped against the stones along the bank and soothed Maggie as she examined the shore line. Nothing. She completed her circuit of the park and casually lifted the lids of two trash cans to glance inside. Nothing.

She headed for her condo but soon realized she needed to visit the ladies' room. She turned back into the park and hurried down the sidewalk past the playground where the two children laughed and dared each other to swing higher.

Maggie entered the ladies' room in a small cinder block building at the far end of the park. This case was going to drive her nuts. Maybe jail would be more peaceful. She washed her hands and wished her mirror image luck. She tossed her paper towel into the trash and started out the door, but a sudden intuition stopped her. She turned back and removed the lid of the garbage can. Under a wadded mound of paper towels,

Maggie found a tan polyester bedspread. She removed it from the trash and unfolded it. Grass stains streaked one side. Maggie gasped. Her heart pounded in her ears.

After calming herself with a few deep breaths, she refolded the bedspread and took it back to her condo. She rocked Chaos for a few minutes to gather her thoughts before she called Jenny. While waiting for Jenny to answer, Maggie looked at the cat purring in her lap. "I taught every form of delinquent little demon there ever was. I'm not afraid of that wimpy woman," she told him.

Chaos twitched his tail and tossed her a doubtful glance.

Jenny picked up the phone.

"I think I have something that belongs to you," Maggie said.

"Oh, what is it?"

"Did you lose a bedspread in the park bathroom?"

Silence lengthened on the line.

"Jenny, are you there?"

"What do you want with me?" The voice was agitated, impatient.

"I just want to talk with you. Can you come over? You see, I've thought about what you said about Chuck never picking up his own socks. He didn't tidy your condo. You did, didn't you?"

"What are you trying to say?"

"I'll keep the bedspread here for you. Will you come and get it?"

Jenny hesitated. "I'll be right there."

***

Confident that Detective Dorsey was staking out her condo, Maggie rocked and petted Chaos while she waited. The cat fell asleep in her lap.

The doorbell rang. "Come in. It's open," Maggie said.

Jenny entered and closed the door behind her. A metallic click told Maggie that her guest had locked the deadbolt behind her.

Maggie continued to rock as Jenny walked into the living room and raised a pistol toward her.

"Hello, Jenny. Why did you do it, and why didn't you hide the bedspread better?" Maggie kept rocking. Chaos awoke and kneaded Maggie's legs as he watched Jenny. He uttered a low, prolonged growl.

"He was leaving me. After all I put up with, he was leaving me." She took a couple of steps closer. "And now, thanks to your prying, I'm going to have to kill you, too. Where's the bedspread?" The hand with the gun shook; Jenny's gaze darted back and forth.

Maggie rocked and nodded toward the couch.

Jenny took two more steps closer, cocked the pistol, and glanced toward the couch.

Chaos sprang onto Jenny's head. He yowled. He dug his front claws into her scalp. He scratched at her eyes with his back claws. Every hair on his enraged body stood on end.

Jenny dropped the gun and flailed at Chaos.

Maggie leapt out of her chair and grabbed the weapon. "Good work, Chaos, good boy."

"Get this damn demon off of me!" Jenny shrieked. She shook her head, staggered, and swatted at the cat, who emitted an unearthly growl, dug in deeper, and slashed Jenny's face. Blood ran down her cheeks. She sank to her knees.

Chaos showed no sign of slowing his attack. He scratched. He spat. He bit. He hissed.

Jenny yanked at him with both hands. She wailed. He dug his claws in deeper still and shrieked like a siren headed to a crime scene. Maggie clutched the gun and retrieved her cell phone. She pointed the pistol at Jenny and called Detective Dorsey. Chaos drew more blood.

When Detective Dorsey burst through the now unlocked door, Maggie again was sitting and rocking. The cat was crouched on the floor facing Jenny, his hair burred like a porcupine, his tail switching, his posture poised to spring. Jenny was sitting in a kitchen chair with her hands tied behind her back and to the chair rungs with a length of blue sateen ribbon. Blood dripped from multiple slashes on her scalp and face. "I killed Chuck," she said. "Just get me away from that damn cat."

Peggy Cartmill Insula

Made in the USA
Columbia, SC
17 October 2024